Verses for Young Readers

by David McCord

FAR AND FEW

TAKE SKY

Take Sky

take
sky

More Rhymes of the Never Was and Always Is

by David McCord

DRAWINGS BY HENRY B. KANE

Little, Brown and Company   *Boston · Toronto*

LIBRARY OF CONGRESS CATALOG CARD NO. 62–12392

Second Printing

Certain of these poems have already appeared in print. I have to thank the
editors of the *Atlantic*, the *Horn Book*, the *New York Times Book Review*,
and the *Boston Globe*.

D. T. W. McC.

*Published simultaneously in Canada
by Little, Brown & Company (Canada) Limited*

PRINTED IN THE UNITED STATES OF AMERICA

To
Ross McCord Miller

Blesséd Lord, what it is to be young:
To be of, to be for, be among —
    Be enchanted, enthralled,
    Be the caller, the called,
The singer, the song, and the sung.

Contents

Take Sky

Take Sky

Now think of words. Take *sky*
And ask yourself just why —
Like sun, moon, star, and cloud —
It sounds so well out loud,
And pleases so the sight
When printed black on white.
Take syllable and thimble:
The sound of *them* is nimble.
Take bucket, spring, and dip
Cold water to your lip.
Take balsam, fir, and pine:
Your woodland smell and mine.
Take kindle, blaze, and flicker —
What lights the hearth fire quicker?

Three words we fear but form:
Gale, twister, thunderstorm;
Others that simply shake
Are tremble, temblor, quake.
But granite, stone, and rock:
Too solid, they, to shock.

3

Put honey, bee, and flower
With sunny, shade, and shower;
Put *wild* with bird and wing,
Put *bird* with song and sing.
Aren't paddle, trail, and camp
The cabin and the lamp?
Now look at words of rest —
Sleep, quiet, calm, and blest;

At words we learn in youth —
Grace, skill, ambition, truth;
At words of lifelong need —
Grit, courage, strength, and deed;
Deep-rooted words that say
Love, hope, dream, yearn, and pray;
Light-hearted words — girl, boy,
Live, laugh, play, share, enjoy.
October, April, June —
Come late and gone too soon.
Remember, words are life:
Child, husband, mother, wife;
Remember, and I'm done:
Words taken one by one

Are poems as they stand —
Shore, beacon, harbor, land;
Brook, river, mountain, vale,
Crow, rabbit, otter, quail;
Faith, freedom, water, snow,
Wind, weather, flood, and floe.
Like light across the lawn
Are morning, sea, and dawn;
Words of the green earth growing —
Seed, soil, and farmer sowing.
Like wind upon the mouth
Sad, summer, rain, and south.
Amen. Put not asunder
Man's *first* word: wonder . . . wonder . . .

Kite

I flew my kite
One bright blue day,
Light yellow-orangey away
Above the tip tall tops of trees,
With little drops from breeze to breeze,
With little rises and surprises,
And the string would sing to these.

I flew my kite
One white new day,
Bright orange-yellowy and gay
Against the clouds. I flew it through
The cloudiness of one or two —
Careering, veering, disappearing;
String to fingers, tight and true.

I flew my kite
One dole-dark day,
Dull orange image in the grey,
When not a single bird would fly
So windy wet and wild a sky
Of little languors and great angers.
Kite, *good-by, good-by, good-by!*

Bananas and Cream

Bananas and cream,
Bananas and cream:
All we could say was
Bananas and cream.

We couldn't say fruit,
We wouldn't say cow,
We didn't say sugar —
We don't say it now.

Bananas and cream,
Bananas and cream,
All we could shout was
Bananas and cream.

We didn't say why,
We didn't say how;
We forgot it was fruit,
We forgot the old cow;
We *never* said sugar,
We only said *WOW!*

Bananas and cream,
Bananas and cream;
All that we want is
Bananas and cream!

We didn't say dish,
We didn't say spoon;
We said not tomorrow,
But NOW and HOW SOON

Bananas and cream,
Bananas and cream?
We yelled for bananas,
Bananas and scream!

Scat! Scitten!

Even though
    a cat has a kitten,
    not a rat has a ritten,
    not a bat has a bitten,
    not a gnat has a gnitten,
    not a sprat has a spritten.
    That is that — that is thitten.

Up the Pointed Ladder

Up the pointed ladder, against the apple tree,
One rung, two rungs, what do I see?
A man by the roadside, his eye on me.

Two rungs, three rungs, and so much higher:
I see five miles to the white church spire.
Bet you that man there wishes he were spryer.

Three rungs, four rungs, holding on tight;
Up near the apples now and ready for a bite.
The man by the roadside — is *he* all right?

Four rungs, five rungs — scary, oh my!
There's not much left but the big blue sky,
The faraway mountains, and a wild man's cry.

Five rungs, six rungs. I guess I'm through.
I seem a little dizzy but the apples are too.
And the man yells "Sonny!" and the cow goes "Moo!"

Seven rungs, eight rungs — I can't climb these.
The wobble's in the ladder, it isn't in my knees.
The man cries "Steady, boy!" And up comes a breeze.

Up comes a breezy "Now you come down slow!"
I offer him an apple, but he just won't go.
Well, it's all like that in the world below.

The Importance of Eggs

I've broken lots of eggs, I guess.
The ones in pockets make a mess,
The ones on floors don't clean up well,
The older ones may leave a smell.
Eggs in a bag when dropped won't splash;
The thrown egg will — a yellow smash.
Big double handfuls from the nest
Are eggs that break the easiest.
All boiled eggs shatter. You can peel
The pieces off. I like the feel
Of peeled boiled eggs, but like the look
Of eggs we neither break nor cook —

These incubator eggs in trays
Behind the glass. Whoever stays
Around to see the chicks peck through
Their shells at hatching time? I do.
Of all egg-breakers, Number One
Is Mr. Chick. When he's begun,
And you can see his little bill
Poke, poke, and figure how he will
Turn round inside his prison-house,
As nimble as a nibbling mouse,
Until he's back where he began:
You'll have respect for eggs, young man.
For then, with one good final kick,
There is no egg, but just a chick.

Tooth Trouble

When I see the dentist
I take him all my teeth:
Some of me's above them,
But most of me's beneath.

And one is in my pocket,
Because it grew so loose
That I could fit a string to it
And tighten up the noose.

I'll grow another, dentist says,
And shall not need to noose it.
Another still to drill and fill?
Not me! I won't produce it.

How Tall?

"How tall?" they say.
"You're taller!" they cry.
He stands in the hall
to measure his tall
new tallness.

　　　　All
they do is to lay
a book on his head
so it's good and square
by the door-jamb where
old pencil marks compare.

Such talk, such bustle!
"Don't *lean* on the door,
Don't move a muscle!"
He doesn't.
He thought that he was taller before.
He wasn't.

Wishful

I'd like to slide my sled to bed
And skate myself to school;
I'd like to tame a crow and show
Him off, and make a rule

That rabbits bark and dogs should twitch
Their noses, and that cats
Should fear a mouse. And if the house
Be flittery with bats,

I'd always want it said *How right*
It is that bats can flitter.
Of course this doesn't fit the facts —
But I'm a poor fact-fitter.

Snowman

My little snowman has a mouth,
So he is always smiling south.
My little snowman has a nose;
I couldn't seem to give him toes,
I couldn't seem to make his ears.
He shed a lot of frozen tears
Before I gave him any eyes —
But they are big ones for his size.

I Want You to Meet . . .

. . . Meet Ladybug,
her little sister Sadiebug,
her mother, Mrs. Gradybug,
her aunt, that nice oldmaidybug,
and Baby — she's a fraidybug.

Food and Drink

1 CUP

"Cup, what's up?
Why, it's cocoa scum!
And who likes that?"
"Some."

2 PLATE

"Plate, there's a great
Deal piled on you."
"I know," says Plate,
"But what can *I* do?"

3 KNIFE AND FORK

"Knife, Fork — look,
You're always together."
"So are shepherd and crook,
Stone and brook,
Fish and hook,
Bell and book,
Kitchen, cook,
Umbrella and rainy weather."

20

4 NAPKIN

"Napkin, you're slipping.
Why have you no talent for gripping?"
"Why have you no lap,
Quiet, where I can nap?"

5 SAUCER

"Saucer, what's for dessert?"

"Don't ask *me!*
I won't be hurt
To stay clear of dessert.
But let's see:
Could be prunes, I guess.
Yes, could be prunes."

"Noon's not the time to have . . . what?"

"I forgot —
I always forget, meal to meal.
Saucers can't *feel*,
We just fill
Or we spill.
Here it comes."

"Golly, *plums!*"

6 TABLE

"Table, I've got my eye on you,
Hoping there may be pie on you.
And if there isn't, fie on you!
Right now there's a fly on you."

7 PITCHER

"Pitcher,
You unreliable switcher
from milk to water to lemonade
which I shall grade:
    1) lemonade
    2) milk
    3) water,
Glass, your daughter,
is asking for you.
Shall I pour you?"

8 JAM

"Spread," said Toast to Butter,
And Butter spread.
"That's better, Butter,"
Toast said.

"Jam," said Butter to Toast.
"Where are you, Jam,
When we need you most?"
Jam: "Here I am,

Strawberry, trickly and sweet.
How are you, Spoon?"
"I'm helping somebody eat,
I think, pretty soon."

9 SALT AND PEPPER

"Why," says Salt to Pepper,
"are we always separate —
I in my cellar;
and you, poor feller,
in a box, mill, or grinder?
It would be kinder
to let you loose."

"No use," says Pepper:
"You take life easy,
I make life sneezy.
Why, damp or dry,
there you lie;
but if I let fly,
people cry."

"I see," says Salt.
"Not your fault,
I suppose.
You're O.K. by me;
so is sugar in tea.
And so it goes.
But then,
I've no nose."

10   JUG AND MUG

"Jug, aren't you fond of Mug?"
"Him I could hug," said Jug.
"Mug, aren't you fond of Jug?"
"Him I could almost slug!"
"Humph," said Jug with a shrug.
"When he pours, he goes *Glug!*" said Mug.
"Well, *I* don't spill on the rug," said Jug.
"Smug old Jug," said Mug.
"I'll fill you, Mug," said Jug.
"*Will*, will you, Jug!" said Mug.
"Don't be ugly," said Jug juggly.
"Big lug," said Mug.
Glug.

So Run Along and Play

You might think I was in the way.
So run along — along with what?
There isn't much that I have got
To run along with or beside.
The door, of course, is open wide;
The day, of course, is clear and fine;
The time right now, I guess, is mine.

But what is there to run to?
It wouldn't be much fun to
Run along — well, just to run.
O.K. for two or three; I'm *one*,
I'm all alone. I guess I'll walk
Along. I'll stop somewhere and talk;
Perhaps I'll think where I can walk to,
Because that's where there's what I'll talk to.
I'll walk along, but I won't play;
I won't play I am playing. Way
Beyond the third house one block back's
Another house with funny cracks
Across the paint. It seems to me
That's where some painter ought to be.

He should have been there years ago;
Maybe they don't like painters, though.
Or maybe he has my complaint:
They said "So run along and paint."
Well, if he ran along like me,
I'll bet I may know where he'll be.

Squaw Talk

I see a lot of cowboys.
Have they ever seen a cow?
I hear a lot of gunfire
In a shabby sort of row,
All answering some podners primed
With something that goes *Pow!*

I see a lot of Indians —
No wigwam or canoe.
And sleepy in my teepee
I am not much likely to,
For squaws who play with Indians
Are very, very few.

Come Christmas snow, while wranglers wear
New chaps and stuff astride
The TV range, in turtleneck
And ski pants far outside,
With twinkly spurs and a bouncy grey,
Through the wide white fields I ride.

Man for Mars

Spaced in a helmet
now his head
still has a mouth
which must be fed,

still has two eyes
for looking round,
still has big ears
but little sound;

still has a nose
that runs a bit —
no spaceman blows
or scratches it;

still has two hands
which he employs
in picking apples;
still enjoys

the heady smell
of autumn air —

especially heady
inside there.

Apples! Some wormy,
mostly beauties.
His inter-
planetary duties

over now, let
Mars and Cygnus-
X relax;
too much of bigness,

too much of all
this interstellar
business tires
a busy feller.

Here is a barn
and here is sun:
a combination
darn good fun;

a spaceman's helmet
full of Macs,

free oxygen
the cosmos lacks;

white teeth, an apple,
the heaven's dome,
and a hornet blasting
off for home.

Sailor John

Young Stephen has a young friend John
Who in his years is getting on.
He's getting on for six, I think,
Or seven. Yes, he's on the brink
Of seven, which is pretty old
Unless you're eight or nine all told.
But anyhow, John has a notion
That he would like to sail the ocean.
He has the notion, understand,
But *not* the ocean — just the land.
John hasn't any boat as yet,
Although his feet are often wet:
They're wet today because of rain.
Quite right — he can't go out again
Unless he finds some other shoes.
John has a notion he will choose
To stay inside and shut the door
And lie right down upon the floor
And think about the ocean, how
It's not available just now;
And think about the kinds of boat
He doesn't have that wouldn't float.

Sing-Song

Clocks
are full of tocks.
When they stop
the trick's
to fix the ticks.
Tick-tock
G'long!
says the clock.

Clip-clop —
that's the horse,
of course.
A flick of the whip
and he goes at a good fast clip.
If his clop goes too,
he hasn't lost a shoe.

Ding!
hear the bell ring?
clapper in the mouth
swinging north and south,
swinging up and down,
ding-dong over the town.
If something's wrong,
it's *always* in the dong.

Where?

Where is that little pond I wish for?
Where are those little fish to fish for?

Where is my little rod for catching?
Where are the bites that I'll be scratching?

Where is my rusty reel for reeling?
Where is my trusty creel for creeling?

Where is the line for which I'm looking?
Where are those handy hooks for hooking?

Where is the worm I'll have to dig for?
Where are the boots that I'm too big for?

Where is there *any* boat for rowing?
Where is . . . ?
                Well, anyway, it's snowing.

You Mustn't Call It Hopsichord

You mustn't call it *hopsichord*,
It's not played by a toad.
You mustn't say a *chevaleer* —
It wasn't he who rode.
It's *sacred* to the memory of,
Not *scared*, as you prefer.
You put apostrophes in *we're*
And keep them out of *were*.
Un*durfed?* No, no, it's under*fed;*
Bed-raggled isn't right, I said.
You *shirr* an egg — how could you shear it?
Music's not hominy or grits;
The thing is *ferret*, though you fear it;
Twist *twist*, and twist is *twits*.
Please never say again you're *mizzled;*
Mis-led you are, or led astray.
The word is wizened and not *wizzled;*
Hens don't lie down — they *lay*.

Spelling Bee

It takes a good speller
to spell *cellar*,
separate, and *benefiting;*
not omitting
cemetery, *cataclysm*,
picknicker and *pessimism*.
And have you ever tried
innocuous, *inoculate*,
dessert, *deserted*, *desiccate;*
divide and *spied*,
gnat, *knickers*, *gnome*,
crumb, *crypt*, and *chrome;*
surreptitious, *supersede*,
delete, *dilate*, *impede?*

GNOME

37

Castor Oil

Ever, ever, not ever so terrible
Stuff as unbearable castor oil
Deep in the glass
Like a chew of cheese,
Like a squeal of brass-bound
Antifreeze.
And round the rim
Of the glass a squeeze
Of orange and lemon.
But will they please
Not say "Delicious!"
And "You won't taste it!"
It's just as vicious
As when *they* faced it.

Three Signs of Spring

Kite on the end of the twine,
Fish on the end of a line,
Dog on the end of a whine.

Dog on the leash is straining,
Fish on the line is gaining:
Only these two complaining.

Kite is all up in the air,
Kite doesn't quite compare,
Kite doesn't *really* care.

Kite, of course, is controllable;
Dog, with a word, consolable;
Fish hopes he isn't poleable.

Trust the dog for an urge,
Trust the kite for a surge,
Trust the trout to submerge.

Kite in the wind and the rain,
Dog in the woods again,
Fish in his deep domain.

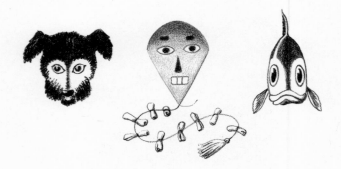

Starling

In burnished armor
with yellow lance
a knighted starling
now perchance

stiff-legged unhorsed
but bold as brass
steps from his stirrups
across the grass.

No guile has he
nor sword nor shield;
he levels with
his lance the field.

Pigeon and sparrow
yield him way
unmailed unequal
each are they;

whatever it is
they pick to peck
Sir Starling will
in person check.

Cold iridescence
in the sun
he sweeps the terrace
with his Begone!

For certes court
and kingdom lie
wherever birds
will flock and fly.

Afreet

Afreet I am afraid of:
I don't know what he's made of.
I don't know where he hides,
Or maybe just abides,
Or maybe has a haunt.
Whatever does he want?
I don't know what he does,
Or if he is or was.
I don't know how he looks;
He's giving me the shooks.
I think he's a jinnee —
You know what *that* would be!
A giant among jinn,
A groan to end a grin,
A shriek to still a sigh,
A croak to kill a cry.
Afreet gives me a fright:
I'm glad he's out of sight.

Alley Cat

His nightly song will scarce be missed:
Nine times death claimed our alley cat.
Good-by, you old somnambulist! —
A long word, that.

Mr. Halloween

He has no broomstick, but you dare not say
Jack Pumpkinhead and he are not old friends.
He has the last word there with Jack — the way
He flickers with Jack's light in candle-ends.

One sheet makes quite a ghost of Tom or Jill;
But Tom and Jill are real and go about
Their night's work putting scare into the shrill
Still younger Toms and Jills who may be out —

Not seeing Mr. Halloween, who bides
His time in some tree's knothole, in some crack
Where *was* a door once: So he often hides
To send the shivers up and down Tom's back.

Or croaks to Jill from nowhere. "Who was that?"
She cries. No . . . nothing . . . nothing . . . all in fun.
But *was* it? Through the shadow flits a bat.
And those two witches! Now there's only *one*.

Sly Mr. Halloween! Don't trust him, Joan.
He's in the dark glass, searching through your mask.

He was that rustle in the leaves, your own
(You *thought* your own) dry voice. Don't ever ask

Strange characters in cloak and hat if they
Are so-and-so, for one may vanish quick
Before your eyes. Be careful how you say
All words that sound like *Boo!* Don't ever lick

The candied apple which he may have seen.
Be wary of those bubbles in a jug
Of cider — just like Mr. Halloween
To be the one you pour into your mug.

Good luck this chancy night! Be sure to wear
Your ring on backwards, or to point your toes
In, *in* — not out — when something skitters. *Scare!*
That's Mr. Halloween. But *when?* Who knows!

Write Me a Verse

I've asked Professor Swigly Brown
To talk about four kinds of Rime,
If you will kindly settle down.
You won't? Well, then, some other time. . . .

PROFESSOR BROWN: The simplest of all verse to write is the couplet. There is no argument about this: it *is* the simplest. I have said so.

Couplet

1

A couplet is two lines — two lines in rime.
The first comes easy, the second may take time.

2

Most couplets will have lines of equal length;
This gives them double dignity and strength.

3

Please count the syllables in 2 and say
How many. Ten each line? Correct! And they

4

In turn comprise the five-foot standard line:
Pentameter. The foot's *iambic.* Fine

5

Enough! On human feet, of course, our shoes
Do match; likewise the laces. If you choose

6

A briefer line,
Like this of mine,

7

Or say
O.K.

8

Why, *these* are couplets, somewhat crude but true
To form. Try one yourself. See how you do.

Meanwhile, I'll give *you* one. Hand me that pen.
A four-foot line — eight syllables, not ten:

10

I cán / not síng / the old / songs nów;
I név / er cóuld / sing án / y hów.

11

Couplets, you see, should make their stand alone.
I've used some differently, but that's my own

12

responsibility.

PROFESSOR BROWN: We come now to the second easiest form of verse: the quatrain. Since the quatrain in length equals *two* couplets, it ought to be just twice as easy to write. It isn't . . . it isn't.

Quatrain

1

When there is more to say — or more than planned —
A couplet's very easy to expand.
Expansive couplets, then, if out of hand,
May nicely run to four lines. Understand?

2

Four lines — quatrain; long lines or short,
But *good* lines, with a good report
Of one another as they progress.
Note one / an oth / er for change / of stress

3

Or emphasis: the sudden sharpening pace.
A quatrain says its say with perfect grace.
"I strove with none, for none was worth my strife" —
First line of four* to haunt you all your life.

---

* Inquire of Walter Savage Landor in *Bartlett's Familiar Quotations*.

4

I'll not attempt a long example —
I mean with lines of many feet;
But still you ought to have a sample
Or two to prove the form *is* neat.

5

Here goes:
Suppose
Suppose
Suppose

6

The ship sails for Spain,
For Spain the ship sails;
You can't go by train,
For a train runs on rails.

7

Let's sail a ship for far-off Spain;
We really can't get there by train.
But still a big ship has no sails;
Why not a train that has no rails?

8

Note rimes in 1 — the rime control is *planned*.
In 2, *two* pairs of rimes; in 6 we find
abab (*Spain, sails, train, rails*). Last kind
Is this (abba): *planned, find, kind, and*

9

Forget that ship that has no sails.
Let's jet by plane across to Spain
Above the sea they call the Main.
(Say something here that rimes with *sails*.)

PROFESSOR BROWN: The limerick, by all odds, is the most
popular short verse form in English.
Hundreds of people write hundreds of
wretched limericks every day. Some-
how they fail to understand that the

54

limerick, to be lively and successful, *must* have *perfect* riming and *flawless* rhythm. The limerick form is far older than Edward Lear (1812-1888), but it was he who first made it popular.

1

A limerick shapes to the eye
Like a small very squat butterfly,
    With its wings opened wide,
    Lots of nectar inside,
And a terrible urge to fly high.

2

The limerick's lively to write:
Five lines to it — all nice and tight.
    Two long ones, two trick
    Little short ones; then quick
As a flash here's the last one in sight.

Some limericks — most of them, reely —
Make rimes fit some key word like *Greely*
    (A man) of *Dubuque*
    (Rimed with cucumber — cuque)
Or a Sealyham (dog). Here it's *Seely*.

There once was a scarecrow named Joel
Who couldn't scare crows, save his soel.
    But the crows put the scare
    Into Joel. He's not there
Any more. That's his hat on the poel.

"There was an old man" of wherever
You like, thus the limerick never
    Accounts for the young:
    You will find him unsung
Whether stupid, wise, foolish, or clever.

6

There was a young man, let me say,
Of West Pumpkinville, Maine, U.S.A.
    You tell me there's not
    Such a place? Thanks a lot.
I forget what he did anyway.

7

Take the curious case of Tom Pettigrew
And Hetty, his sister. When Hettigrew
    As tall as a tree
    She came just to Tom's knee.
And did *Tom* keep on growing? You bettigrew.

8

Consider this odd little snail
Who lives on the rim of a pail:
    Often wet, never drowned,
    He is always around
Safe and sound, sticking tight to his trail.

9

A man who was fond of his skunk
Thought he smelled pure and pungent as punk.
    But his friends cried No, no,
      No, no, no, no, no, *no!*
He just stinks, or he stank, or he stunk.

10

There was an old man who cried Boo!
Not to me or to he but to you.
    He also said scat
    To a dog not a cat,
And to Timbuc he added too-too.

11

It's been a bad year for the moles
Who live just in stockings with holes;
    And bad for the mice
    Who prefer their boiled rice
Served in shoes that don't have any soles.

12

There once was a man in the Moon,
But he got there a little too soon.
   Some others came later
   And fell down a crater —
When *was* it? Next August? Last June?

13

"This season our tunnips was red
And them beets was all white. And instead
   Of green cabbages, what
   You suspect that we got?"
"I don't know." "Didn't plant none," he said.

14

I don't much exactly quite care
For these cats with short ears and long hair;
   But if anything's worse
   It's the very reverse:
Just you ask any mouse anywhere.

So by chance it may be you've not heard
Of a small sort of queer silent bird.
    Not a song, trill, or note
    Ever comes from his throat.
If it does, I take back every word.

16

Write a limerick now. Say there was
An old man of some place, what he does,
    Or perhaps what he doesn't,
    Or isn't or wasn't.
Want help with it? Give me a buzz.

PROFESSOR BROWN: The triolet is another brief verse form, no longer popular and not too easy to write, even though it *looks* easy. The rime-scheme (end words) is abaaabab. That is, in example 1 the rimes will repeat in that order:

droll	(a)	soul	(a)
repeat	(b)	feet	(b)
control	(a)	droll	(a)
droll	(a)	repeat	(b)

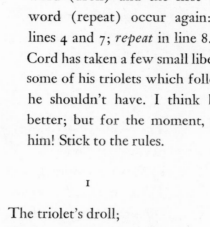

Please observe that the first (a) rime-word (droll) and the first (b) rime-word (repeat) occur again: *droll* in lines 4 and 7; *repeat* in line 8. Mr. Mc-Cord has taken a few small liberties with some of his triolets which follow — but he shouldn't have. I think he knows better; but for the moment, shame on him! Stick to the rules.

1

The triolet's droll;
You must watch it repeat
The lines in control.
The triolet's droll
With a brightness of soul,
With such swift little feet!
The triolet's droll;
You must watch it repeat.

2

The birds in the feeder
are fighting again.
Not squirrels in the cedar,

but birds in the feeder.
They haven't a leader:
just eight, nine, or ten
of the birds in the feeder
are fighting again.

3

The swallows all twitter
In line on the wire.
Each fatter and fitter,
The swallows all twitter:
Old sitter, young sitter,
Madáme and Esquíre.
The swallows all twitter
In line on the wire.

4

Eggs are all runny,
Though legs they have none.
It's terribly funny
That eggs are all runny!
When laid by a bunny
For Easter, not one

Of *his* eggs are all runny:
They roll and *we* run.

5

It's a foggy day
When winter thaws
And the snow is grey.
It's a foggy day:
O Doggy, go 'way
With your dirty paws!
It's a foggy day
When winter thaws.

6

I fed some cheese
To the cellar mice.
It went like a breeze
When I fed some cheese;
And they came by threes
And they came in a trice
When I fed some cheese
To the cellar mice.

Thank you, thank you, Professor Brown!
You've made us feel all upside down,
All inside out, all backside to —
But that's what you are paid to do.

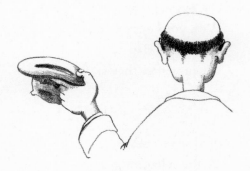

A Fool and His Money

Looking back over the years,
Nothing now seems so sad,
So much a matter of tears,
As the little gold piece I had:
Gold piece and a five-dollar bill,
And tell you of them I will.

The little gold piece was small,
Worth five times fifty cents;
You may say it was nothing at all,
But to me oh, immense, immense.
And it was; for what else indeed
Could I ever want or need?

One little gold piece the size
Of a penny — there aren't any now —
And deep in the pocket to prize.
So I remember how

And where and exactly when,
When I was twelve or ten,

In the observation car
Of our California train
I sat out back; and far
Behind me slid the plain.
And what would become of me
In the land where I was to be?

I tossed a penny to see:
Heads for a happy life.
"What would become of me?"
Went through me like a knife.
A penny flew into space.
What penny! No trace, no trace.

It was like the five-dollar bill
Before we took to the West.
Aunt Mary: I see her still
At the station, departing guest,
With a crisp new five and a kiss.
But in my delirious bliss

I ran up and down till (the train
Coming in) I was caught by the hand,
And the bill made a green little stain
In the steam and the wind. I must stand
And wait till the train took Aunt Mary.
Five dollars? No trace — nary, nary.

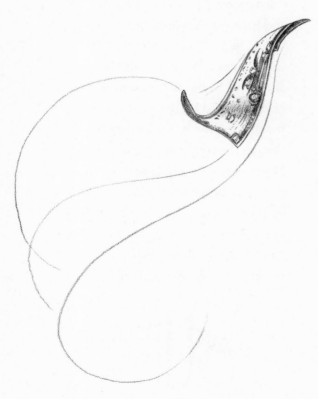

I Have a Book

that has no cover
where there used to be a lady
and her knighted lover.
Oh, her lover was a knight
and his armor fitted right.
While he hadn't any horse,
still I always thought he might;
and I always thought of course
he'd be riding far away,
for the day was good and bright
though the tree was big and shady.
Now there isn't any lady
and there isn't any knight,
and there never was a horse,
so there never was a fight.
And the book all by itself
is sort of lonely on the shelf.

Sally Lun Lundy

Barefoot Monday
For Sally Lun Lundy;
Stocking-day, shoes-day
All day Tuesday.
A rather loose-ends day
Turns up Wednesday.
Not-a-leaf-stirs-day
Well through Thursday.
Lowest low-tide-day
Wading on Friday.
Solemn old Saturday:
Raindrops-splatter-day.

What about Sunday,
Sally Lun Lundy?

Mingram Mo

There was a man named Mingram Mo
Who never knew just where to go.
Mo had a friend — I forget his name —
Who never knew from whence he came.
And then Mo's sister, Mrs. Kriss,
Would misremember most of this,
And say to Mingram: "Mingram Mo,
What is it that you never know?
And who's this friend who knows it less?"
(His name still slips me, I confess.)
Whereat poor Mingram would invent
A place to go to when he went,
Wherein his friend called — never mind —
Might feel quite not so left behind.
But where *that* was, his sister Mrs.
Kriss still misremembers. This is
All that you will ever know of
Mingram Mo, by Jove, by Jo-of.

Down by the Sea

Everybody's in the ocean,
Everybody's gone to sail;
Everybody's rubbing lotion.
Where is Johnny? Here's his pail.

Every kind of beach umbrella,
Every sort of bouncy ball;
Johnny wades an archipela-
go of rocky islands, all

Razored barnacles as thickly
Spread as freckles on your face.
Johnny doesn't care partickly,
Splashing Sammy's sister Grace;

Or it may be Sammy's brother —
Down by the sea they're much the same.
Someone's aunt is someone's mother,
No one's dad is glad he came.

Every boy has dug a tunnel,
Built a castle, buried Pop;
Every girl thinks Oh, what fun'll
I have barefoot — slop, slop, slop!

Everybody's wet and sandy,
Everybody's fat or thin;
Johnny lets his soggy candy
Drip and dribble down the chin.

Every picnic spot is where a
Youngster running by can spread
Something of the soft Sahara
Over something that was bread.

Everybody's got a tiny
Radio that blares the news;
Everybody beached or briny
Sweats or shivers, smokes or chews.

Everybody's Coke is fizzy,
Everybody's towel is damp.
See where Johnny's . . . O.K., is he?
I *can't* turn: I've got a cramp.

Everybody's hallelujah
Isn't everybody's dish.
Everybody, then: here's to ya,
Johnny's found a stinking fish.

Queer

I seem to see
in the apple tree,
I seem to know
from the field below,
I seem to hear
when the woods are near,
I seem to sense
by the farmer's fence,
I seem to place
just the faintest trace,
I seem to smell
what I can't quite tell,
I seem to feel
that it isn't real,
I seem to guess
at it, more or less.

Alphabet

(Eta Z)

1

A is one
And we've begun.

2

B is two —
Myself and you.

3

C is three —
You, who? and me.

4

D is four;
Let's close the door.

5

E is five
Bees in a hive.

6

F is six
Fat candlesticks.

7

G is seven
And not eleven.

8

H is eight,
And gaining weight.

9

I is nine,
Of slender spine;

10

J is ten.
And then what? Then

11

Comes K eleven
Which isn't seven.

12

L is twelve,
Or two-thirds elve.

13

M thirteen
Stands in between

14

Your A, my Z.
N's fourteen. We

15

Now come to O;
Fifteen or so —

16

Fifteen, I guess;
P Sixteen. Yes,

17

Since seventeen
Cries Q for Queen!

18

Eighteen is R,
The end of star;

19

Nineteen is S
As in success;

20

T's twenty, twice
What ten was; nice

21

To add one to
And capture U,

22

Or add a pair
That V can share.

23

Your twenty-three's
In wow! Xerxes

24

Shows X the core
Of twenty-four.

25

Y keeps alive
In twenty-five;

26

Z's in a fix:
Poor twenty-six!

What Molly Blye Said

"Look, can you cook?"
Said Mary Brooke.

"Why, I can fry,"
Said Molly Blye.

"*You:* can you stew?"
Said Janet Crewe.

"I? I can fry,"
Said Molly Blye.

"Cake! Can you bake?"
Said Alice Blake.

"Pie? I can fry,".
Said Molly Blye.

"*Boil!* . . . Can't you broil?"
Said Doris Doyle.

"Why? I can fry,"
Said Molly Blye.

"Shirr, can you shirr?"
Said Polly Burr.

(Sigh.) "I can fry,"
Said Molly Blye.

"*Toast!* Can't you roast?"
Said Thelma Post.

"Fry — I can fry,"
Said Molly Blye.

"Poach — if I coach?"
Said Sybil Roach.

"Why, I can try,"
Said Molly Blye.

"Good-by, good-by,
Poor Molly Blye.

Good-by,"
Said I.

Snake

Very thin
and opaque
is the skin
of a snake.

Let it shed,
Let it wane
to this dead
cellophane.

Let it be:
I've no itch
to see
which is which.

Up from Down Under

The boomerang and kangaroo
comprise a very pleasant two;
The coolibah and billabong
together make a sort of song.
But tasty as a fresh meringue
is billabong with boomerang;
and better than hooray-hoorah
is kangaroo with coolibah.

The Cove

The cove is where the swallows skim
And where the trout-rings show,
And where the bullfrog hugs the rim
Of lily pads; and so
The million wake, as hatching flies
Hatch out into a world of eyes,
A world of wing and mouth and fin,
Of feathers, scales, and froggy skin.

A tough old world that *they* are in!

Glowworm

Never talk down to a glowworm —
Such as *What do you knowworm?*
How's it down belowworm?
Guess you're quite a slowworm.
No. Just say
         Helloworm!

Goose, Moose & Spruce

Three gooses: geese.
Three mooses: meese?
Three spruces: spreece?

Little goose: gosling.
Little moose: mosling?
Little spruce: sprosling?

Dr. Klimwell's Fall

(A poem to be read aloud)

> We wake and find our-
> selves on a stair; there
> are stairs below us . . .
> there are stairs above us,
> many a one, which go
> upward and out of sight.
> — RALPH WALDO EMERSON

Down the star-stairs fell
Old Dr. I. Klimwell.
What he was doing there,
Climbing that kind of stair,
Staring down starry stone,
Standing (trust him) alone,
No one will ever know.
Stars, when you have to go
Where Dr. Klimwell did,
Hide away — hidden, hid
Under some stellar door;
But, if you've been before
(Doctors, of course, *have* been)
Knock, and they'll let you in.

Going up, going down
Clean through the heart of town,
Up through the cloudy rug,
Down through the cave undug,
Right where you want to stop;
Star-stairs to bottom, top —
Either way, there they are,
Stairs of the stepping-star.

Old Dr. Klimwell, he —
Much, very much like me;
Much, very much as you —
Liked the same things you do:
People afloat on rafts,
Dust in the sunlit shafts
Shining through colored panes,
Little dogs not on chains,
Little boys out for trout,
Little girls flumped about,
Stores where they sell you stuff,
Seas when they aren't too rough,
Kites when they scrape the sky,
Trees when the leaves let fly;
Trains coming round the curve,
Indians in reserve,

Dolls with their shoes laced right,
Whistles blown late at night —
Whistles one *ought* to hear
When Dr. Klimwell's near —
Lanterns and shouting men,
Roosters but not the hen,
Ducks on the pond; long lakes,
Snowfall in fat wet flakes,
Circuses, clowns, and stunts,
Hands that you held to once,
Holes in the dead tree trunk,
Stones down the well *kerplunk*,
Moss round a mountain bog,
Leopard frogs, bull frogs, frog;
Sodas with triple straws,
Crows with black throaty *caws*,
Rabbits — with twitchy nose,
Places where no one goes;
Birches to climb and swing,
Geese in the sky for spring,
Feel of wet sand on feet,
Dusk down a city street;
Things worlds and winds away
Turning up night and day,

Turning up soon or late,
Turning up while you wait.

Well, that is quite a list
(Not very much I've missed)
Made so you'll understand
What Dr. Klimwell *and*
You and I think about
All day in, all day out.
Little things, some would say.
Happy things, though, *aren't* they?

"There now, at last!" would cry
Old Dr. Klimwell. "My,
My, my, my, *my!* I smell
Leaves burning. Must be well
On towards . . . eh? . . . Halloween?
What is there in between?"
"Nothing. For someone's sick.
Climb, Dr. Klimwell, *quick!*"
Who could be sick above
Whom we'd be thinking of
Not knowing why or where
One could be sick up there?
Quick as the flight of thieves

94

Right by the rake of leaves,
Spiraling through the clear
Leaf-empty trees appear
Stones for the Doctor's climb
Time after sudden time,
Just when your laggard glance
Spies, as it will by chance,
Something you want to see:
Dragonflies floating knee-
High over sandy shore;
Something behind the door,
Something inside of tents,
Something that won't make sense,
Something before your face,
Something from outer space,
Something you've heard of, just —
Something the rain might rust,
Something you don't quite trust,
Something . . .

Many Crows, Any Owl

Caw, caw, *caw!* . . .
Come see them fly.
There's an owl up there
In the tree nearby:

In the big lone oak
With its leaves all brown,
Where the caw-caw-*caws*
Call the old owl down.

But the old owl sits
Till he drops one lid
Over one wide eye:
"Which is *what* I did?"

"Which is you're an owl
Same as we are crows."
So the cause of the caw-caw-
Caws, he goes

To another tree
Near another farm.

There's another great big black
Fresh alarm.

"Oh, but no you don't,"
Says the owl this time.
"There's a man with a gun,
And a crow is prime

"Good reason why
He is out just now,
When he might be thinking
About the cow,

"Or about the calf,
Or the five big geese,
Or the pumpkins just
Up the road a piece.

"But he's after *you*
And your caw-caw noise.
So I'm going to sleep.
Good morning, boys!"

Crickets

all busy punching tickets,
clicking their little punches.
The tickets come in bunches,
good for a brief excursion,
good for a cricket's version
of travel (before it snows) to
the places a cricket goes to.
Alas! the crickets sing alas
in the dry September grass.
Alas, alas, in every acre,
every one a ticket-taker.

The Leaves

When the leaves are young,
Shaped to the tip of tongue,
They do not speak at all.

All summer, green and spread
Sun-dappled overhead,
They talk . . . talk on and on . . .

On days of gentle weather
They whisper, tongues together,
Breathe, meditate, and stir.

Were ever clouds so sure
That clouds will long endure?
Not ever, leaves say. No.

No matter what? In rain
The dripping-leaf refrain
Repeats the pretty patter:

No matter, matter . . . Storm
Takes leaves like bees in swarm —
The sullen swirl in flight.

Light tongues, so bidden bold,
Sting, quiver, lash, and scold.
No matter matter what,

Not death for us, they cry!
But by and by and by
Comes autumn loping lean

Between the woods and village.
Red, yellow, gold, her pillage . . .
The sickled fingers . . . Down

Down flutters every leaf,
Too aerial for grief:
Dead as the unstruck gong.

Long after twirl and spin,
Deleted, spare, and thin
In multiple retreat,

Feet rustle them. We rake
And burn them for the sake
Of dwelling in their smoke.

101

Oh kindle, day of days,
Unbroken blue in haze
The bitter burning sweet:
Sweet burning in our street.

What Am I Up To?

"I'll be right there," says the little man. Please note
He doesn't say "I'll be *left* there" — with his hat and coat.
"I'll be round soon," says the little man. He's thin as a rail.
"What am I in for?" he asks again, though he's not in jail.
"Will you help me out?" now he wants to know.
With a rope? A stepladder? With *what?*
                                        Hello!
"I'm coming down with measles," says the man's little son.
Oh, stay upstairs and have 'em, or come down with just one.

After Christmas

There were lots on the farm,
But the turkeys are gone.
They were gobbling alarm:
There were lots on the farm,
Did they come to some harm,
Like that poor little fawn?
There were lots on the farm,
But the turkeys are gone.

Just Because . . .

Kittens have paws they don't have pawses,
Lions have maws they don't have mawses,
Tigers have jaws they don't have jawses,
And crows have caws they don't have cawses.

I make one pause, I make two pauses:

Nine jackdaws aren't nine jackdawses,
Seven seesaws aren't seven seesawses,
Five oh pshaws aren't five oh pshawses,
Three heehaws aren't three heehawses.

Do you give two straws? Do you give two strawses?

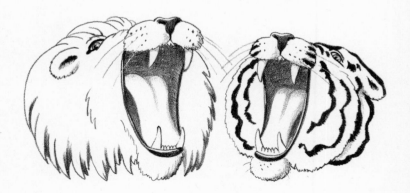

Now Say Good Night

Now say Good Night
they say Now say Good
Night O.K. I say all right
I'll say Good Nights all day
for spite I say I might
Why *Good?* What's Good
about it? Good? I doubt it
Light is better than Night good
or bad all bright the world
the sight of birds in flight
of winter snowy white Now
say good good good good good
night good night good night
good sleepy tight sleep tight
Now say Good Night